POCKETFUL OF NONSENSE

By James Marshall

Houghton Mifflin Company

Boston 2003

Compilation, "A Porker from East Chutney, Wales," "A Tomcat in Fine Tenor Voice," "A Bulldog Was Watching His Weight," "Antoinette Leach Came in from the Beach," and "A Sinister Spider Named Ruth" © 1992 James Marshall. Illustrations © 1992 James Marshall. Originally published by Western Publishing Company, Inc., Racine, Wisconsin 53404.

www.houghtonmifflinbooks.com

Library of Congress Cataloging-in-Publication Data
Pocketful of nonsense / [compiled and illustrated] by James Marshall.
p. cm.
Summary: Old favorites and original works by Marshall make up this collection of humorous rhymes, limericks, and poems.
PAP ISBN 0-618-34186-2 RNF ISBN 0-618-34187-0
1. Children's poetry. 2. Nonsense verses. 3. Limericks. Juvenile. [1. Humorous poetry. 2. Poetry—Collections.] I. Marshall, James, 1942–1992.
PN6109.97.P62 1993
398.8–dc20 93-18297 CIP AC

Manufactured in Mexico

SCP   10 9 8 7 6 5 4 3 2 1

Table of Contents

Fuzzy Wuzzy was a bear,
Fuzzy Wuzzy had no hair,
Fuzzy Wuzzy wasn't fuzzy,
was he?

What's so funny?

There was a young man of Bengal
who went to a fancy-dress ball.
   He went, just for fun,
   dressed up as a bun,
and a dog ate him up in the hall.

There was an old man of Blackheath
who sat on his set of false teeth.
  Said he with a start,
  "Oh Lord, bless my heart!
I've bitten myself underneath!"

Jack Hall,
he is so small
a mouse could eat him,
hat and all.

Cinderella,
dressed in yella,
went upstairs
to kiss her fella,
made a mistake and kissed a snake.
How many doctors did it take?

A porker from East Chutney, Wales,
bespattered his top hat and tails.
　　Now bear this in mind
　　that clothes make the swine,
but mudbaths are good for what ails.
　　　　　—J.M.

A tomcat in fine tenor voice
sang out in the church of his choice,
  "When the service is through
  I will dine on mouse stew.
For this I do truly rejoice."
    —J.M.

A peanut sat on a railroad track.
His heart was all a-flutter.
The five-fifteen came rushing by—
Toot! Toot! Peanut butter!

Through the teeth
and past the gums—
look out, stomach,
here it comes!

A bulldog was watching his weight.
He watched and he watched while he ate.
   "It defies understanding
   why I keep expanding,"
he said as he licked clean his plate.
                    —J.M.

A gentleman dining at Crewe
found quite a large mouse in his stew.
   Said the waiter, "Don't shout
   and wave it about,
or the rest will be wanting one, too!"

I love you, I love you,
I love you divine.
Please give me your bubble gum—
you're *sitting* on mine!

Get up, get up, you lazy head.
Get up, you lazy sinner.
We need those sheets for tablecloths.
It's nearly time for dinner.

Antoinette Leach came in from the beach
with a lobster asleep in her curls.
  Said her mother, "My dear,
  it's perfectly clear,
you're simply not like other girls."
  —J.M.

A sinister spider named Ruth
set up a photography booth.
    In clever disguise
    she'd lure juicy flies
who too late would discover the truth.
    —J.M.

There was an old man of Peru
who dreamed he was eating his shoe.
  He woke in the night
  in a terrible fright
and found it was perfectly true.

There was a young man of Devizes
whose ears were of different sizes.
    The one that was small
    was no use at all,
but the other won several prizes.

Tra la!

I'm so impressed

A horse and a flea and three blind mice
sat on a curbstone shooting dice.
The horse, he slipped and fell on the flea.
The flea said, "Whoops, there's a horse on me."

I asked my mother for fifty cents
to see the elephant jump the fence.
He jumped so high that he touched the sky
and never came back till the Fourth of July.

Teddy Bear, Teddy Bear,
turn around.
Teddy Bear, Teddy Bear,
touch the ground.
Teddy Bear, Teddy Bear,
show your shoe.
Teddy Bear, Teddy Bear,
that will do.

IMAGINE A CITY

❖ Elise Hurst ❖

DOUBLEDAY BOOKS FOR YOUNG READERS

Imagine a train to take you away

Imagine a city
and drops of rain

A world
without edges

Where the wind takes you high

Where buses are fish

and the fish fly the sky

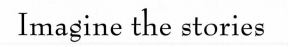

Imagine the stories

and measureless treasure

Where you sit with me
as the gargoyles sip tea

The world is your teacher

The past carries on

and sunlight is breathed
in a murmuring song

Imagine the wonders
of just such a land

Imagine it all
in the palm of your hand.

To Archie and Sam and Peter. I can't wait for us to explore
the world together—just imagine what lies ahead. —E.H.

Copyright © 2014 by Elise Hurst

All rights reserved. Published in the United States by Doubleday, an imprint of
Random House Children's Books, a division of Penguin Random House LLC, New York.
Originally published by Omnibus Books, an imprint of Scholastic Australia Pty Ltd,
Sydney, Australia, in 2014.

Doubleday and the colophon are registered trademarks of
Penguin Random House LLC.

Visit us on the Web! randomhousekids.com

Educators and librarians, for a variety of teaching tools,
visit us at RHTeachersLibrarians.com

Library of Congress Cataloging-in-Publication Data
is available upon request.

ISBN 978-1-101-93457-9 (trade) — ISBN 978-1-101-93458-6 (ebook)

The illustrations in this book were created using pen and ink on paper.

MANUFACTURED IN CHINA
10 9 8 7 6 5 4 3 2 1
First American Edition